WITH ENDLESS GRATITUDE & LOVE TO
GURI SISSEL, ANJA, AND CHERYL

*Many thanks to Mallory & Maria, and to our family, friends,
and readers for their enthusiasm, support, and encouragement.
Special thanks to the Fabulous Cousins, Hanna & Petter, and to Jotne.*

Book Designer: Cheryl Meyer
Digital Artists: Per Breiehagen and Brad Palm

Text copyright © 2015 by Lori Evert
Jacket and interior photographs copyright © 2015 by Per Breiehagen

All rights reserved. Published in the United States by Random House Children's Books,
a division of Random House LLC, a Penguin Random House Company, New York.

Random House and the colophon are registered trademarks of Random House LLC.

Visit us on the Web! randomhousekids.com

Educators and librarians, for a variety of teaching tools, visit us at RHTeachersLibrarians.com

Library of Congress Cataloging-in-Publication Data
Evert, Lori.
The tiny wish / by Lori Evert ; photographs by Per Breiehagen. — First edition.
pages   cm.
Summary: "Anja makes a wish to become small during a game of hide-and-seek—
and her wish comes true! Or does it?" —Provided by publisher.
ISBN 978-0-385-37922-9 (trade) — ISBN 978-0-375-97336-9 (lib. bdg.) — ISBN 978-0-375-98237-8 (ebook)
[1. Voyages and travels—Fiction. 2. Wishes—Fiction. 3. Size—Fiction. 4. Animals—Fiction.]
I. Breiehagen, Per, illustrator. II. Title.
PZ7.E927Tin 2015 [E]—dc23 2014012401

MANUFACTURED IN CHINA   10 9 8 7 6 5 4 3 2 1
First Edition

the TINY Wish

By Lori Evert

Photographs by Per Breiehagen

Random House  New York

Long, long ago, in the days when you could only see as
much of the world as a horse could take you, lived a curious
little girl named Anja.

It was spring, and the snow had melted in all but
the highest places, so Anja reluctantly put her skis away.
Now she envied the butterflies and birds as they swooped
over the mountains and valleys, as she had flown over
the snow.

$\mathcal{A}$nja cheered up when her father took her to visit her cousins at their mountain farm. They lived there through the spring and summer so their sheep and goats could graze in the endless fields.

Springtime in the mountains
is like a bright and lively party; the
rushing streams sing as they escape
the frozen snow, flowers burst forth,
and baby animals chirp, chatter,
and wrestle in the new grass. It is a
magical time when most anything
can happen.

Anja especially liked to ride with her cousins on their giant horse to help them check on the family's goats.

It didn't take long to find the goats; they ran to greet the children when they heard their voices, and eagerly followed them as they looked for the rest of the herd.

After the goats had all been accounted for, the children began to play hide-and-seek. But Anja had a problem: her favorite goat kid was following her. Usually she loved when he tagged along, but he wouldn't hide, so her cousins always found her right away.

"Oh, I wish I could shrink and be so small that no one could find me," she said to herself as she hid behind a big rock.

"What are you waiting for?" asked a tiny voice. Anja looked over and saw a bright-eyed finch staring up at her. "Come down and I'll give you a ride," he said. "Hurry. I hear your cousin coming!"

The next thing Anja knew, she was surrounded by grass as tall as trees and she was looking up at the bird. Her wish had come true!

$\mathcal{A}$nja climbed onto the finch's back and away they flew, over the river and the fields of cotton grass, past her cousins and the goats.

Anja watched in wonder as each familiar thing in the landscape below became smaller and smaller.

After a while, Anja began to get hungry, so the bird brought her to a strawberry patch. The wild strawberries, usually almost too small to taste, were now huge and delicious. It was hot in the sun, so Anja picked a leaf of lady's mantle and made a hat for shade.

She was just about to pluck another strawberry when a yellow bird landed beside them. "Stop picking my berries!" he squawked. Then he snapped the fruit right out of the finch's beak.

As the birds squabbled, Anja noticed her cousins' horse grazing nearby, and she decided it would be exciting to ride on his mane.

She ran over to him, pushing her way through the forest of tall grasses and weeds, past a shiny beetle, and yelled the horse's name.

He couldn't hear her above his loud chewing, so Anja decided to climb up his leg. She scurried around his enormous, crunching teeth and grabbed his fetlock.

The horse must have felt a tickle or a pull, because he suddenly began to run. Anja held tight as she bounced up and down.

*F*inally, the horse slowed. Anja's hands were tired from holding on, so she let go. She tumbled onto a soft, mossy log and landed next to a pinecone.

Then she heard a muffled voice.

"Madam," it said, "please move aside so that I may breathe." Anja shifted her skirt and saw a glistening brown snail. The snail slid his head out of his shell and said, "Much better. Would you be so kind as to help me get home? Climb aboard this pinecone, give it a push, and we will soon be near my stream."

$\mathscr{H}$ave you ever ridden your sled over a jump? If you have, you know how Anja felt as the pinecone slid faster and faster down the log and flew into the air, finally landing in a clump of wet grass.

The snail led Anja to the water's edge. He thanked her for the ride; then he withdrew under a patch of thistle.

Anja loved to swim, so she waded into the water. It was colder, faster, and deeper than ever, now that she was so small. "I can't swim in this!" she said. She sat on a rock and wondered what to do next.

"Let's make a boat!" said a baby squirrel. He jumped down from a tree and landed next to her. "It will be fun!"

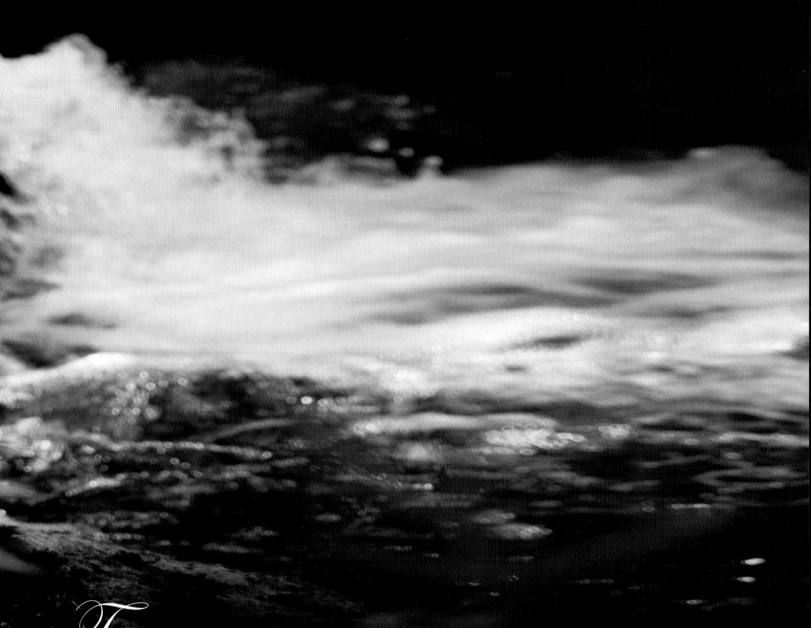

They found a perfect piece of birch bark, then lined it with moss and decorated it with buttercups and starflowers. As they worked, Anja admired the squirrel's nimble paws and squeaky song.

"It's fun to work on a little boat
With a friend with light, long hair.
When you meet a new friend who needs a boat,
It's good to be right there."

When the boat was finished, they dragged it to the water and the squirrel held it as Anja climbed in. She had hoped her friend would join her, but his mother was calling, so they said goodbye.

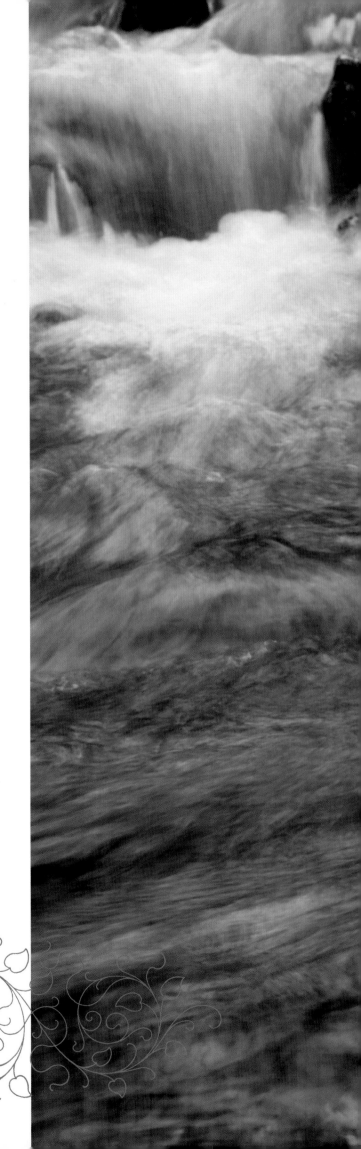

As soon as the squirrel let
go, the boat caught the current
and swirled madly around. Anja
pushed it to calmer water and
began to enjoy her ride.

   She passed a busy anthill that
was dizzy with activity, jungles of
bright ferns, and massive roots
of willow and birch trees. She
was staring in wonder at the fuzzy
wings of a giant butterfly when it
called to her, "Look out!"

*S*uddenly she was caught in some rapids, and the water in
front of her seemed to disappear!

"Waterfall!" the butterfly called. "Jump!"

Anja sprang up, grabbed a branch, and watched as her boat
crashed below.

It's a good thing Anja was an experienced climber; she
inched along the branch, hand over hand, until she reached
land. The butterfly flew to her.

"How frightening!" the butterfly exclaimed. "Follow me.
I have some friends who can assist you if you wish to go home."

$\mathcal{A}$nja scrambled along the rocky edge of the stream and was met by a brood of ducklings, who were quite surprised to see such a tiny human. They began quacking all at once, so she could not understand a word they said.

"Quiet, darlings," said their mother as she waddled up to Anja. "If you could travel by water, you would be very close to where the goats gather. But since the stream is so fast and rocky, you must travel by land. The butterfly is looking for someone to help you."

Anja heard a rustle in the grass and
saw a pair of eyes, then two pairs, then six.
Bunnies! Anja loved bunnies, but she had
never been able to get close to one. Now that
they were larger than she was, they hopped
right up to her.

"You look cold," said one of the bunnies.
"Would you like to warm up next to my fur?"

Anja hugged the bunny. His deep fur was
soft and cozy and smelled like dandelions.

"Children, I must take the little girl
home," said the mother rabbit. "Wait here
with Mother Duck and I'll be back in a hop."
Anja gently pushed through the crowd of
bunnies and climbed onto the mother's back.

*A*nja clutched the rabbit's fur as they bounded down the meadow.

The animals they passed stopped their chewing, their digging, and their conversations to stare at the spectacle.

Finally, they saw the goat kid.
"Anja! You're so tiny! And
you look very tired," he said.
"Wait here and I'll bring your
cousins to you."

Anja lay down on a soft patch
of moss, and the mother rabbit
covered her with cotton grass.

"Close your eyes," she said.
"When you wake, you will be safe
at home."

The next thing Anja knew, she was in her cousin's bed. "My goodness," she thought. "What a curious dream!"

She pushed the blanket back and was amazed to see that the bed was covered with tufts of cotton grass and flowers. "Maybe it *wasn't* a dream!" she said to herself.

What do you think?